HELLO, HEDGEHOG! ™

Let's Go Swimming!

Norm Feuti

ACORN™
SCHOLASTIC INC.

For Charlie and Parker — NF

Library of Congress Cataloging-in-Publication Data
Names: Feuti, Norman, author, illustrator. | Feuti, Norman. Hello, Hedgehog! ; 4.
Title: Let's go swimming! / Norm Feuti.
Description: New York : Acorn/Scholastic inc., 2021. | Series: Hello,
Hedgehog! ; 4 | Summary: On a hot day, Hedgehog and his best friend, Harry,
go swimming in the pond to cool off—and when Hedgehog helps his friend
overcome his fear of going underwater, they find a treasure.
Identifiers: LCCN 2020030126 | ISBN 9781338677119 (paperback) |
ISBN 9781338677126 (library binding) | ISBN 9781338677133 (ebook)
Subjects: LCSH: Hedgehogs—Juvenile fiction. | Swimming—Juvenile fiction. |
Best friends—Juvenile fiction. | CYAC: Hedgehogs—Fiction. |
Swimming—Fiction. | Best friends—Fiction. | Friendship—Fiction.
Classification: LCC PZ7.1.F52 Ld 2021 | DDC [E]—dc23
LC record available at https://lccn.loc.gov/2020030126

10 9 8 7 6 5 4 3 2 1   21 22 23 24 25

Printed in China   62
First edition, May 2021
Edited by Katie Carella
Book design by Maria Mercado

A Hot Day

It is **so** hot today!

I need a way to keep cool.

Maybe the fan will help.

3

But now I am bored.

I need a way to keep cool that is more fun.

4

5

Harry and I can go swimming!

I know just what to bring!

Hmm. Do I need anything else?

I did forget **one** thing.

Swimming

It is a good day for a swim!

Let's have some fun!

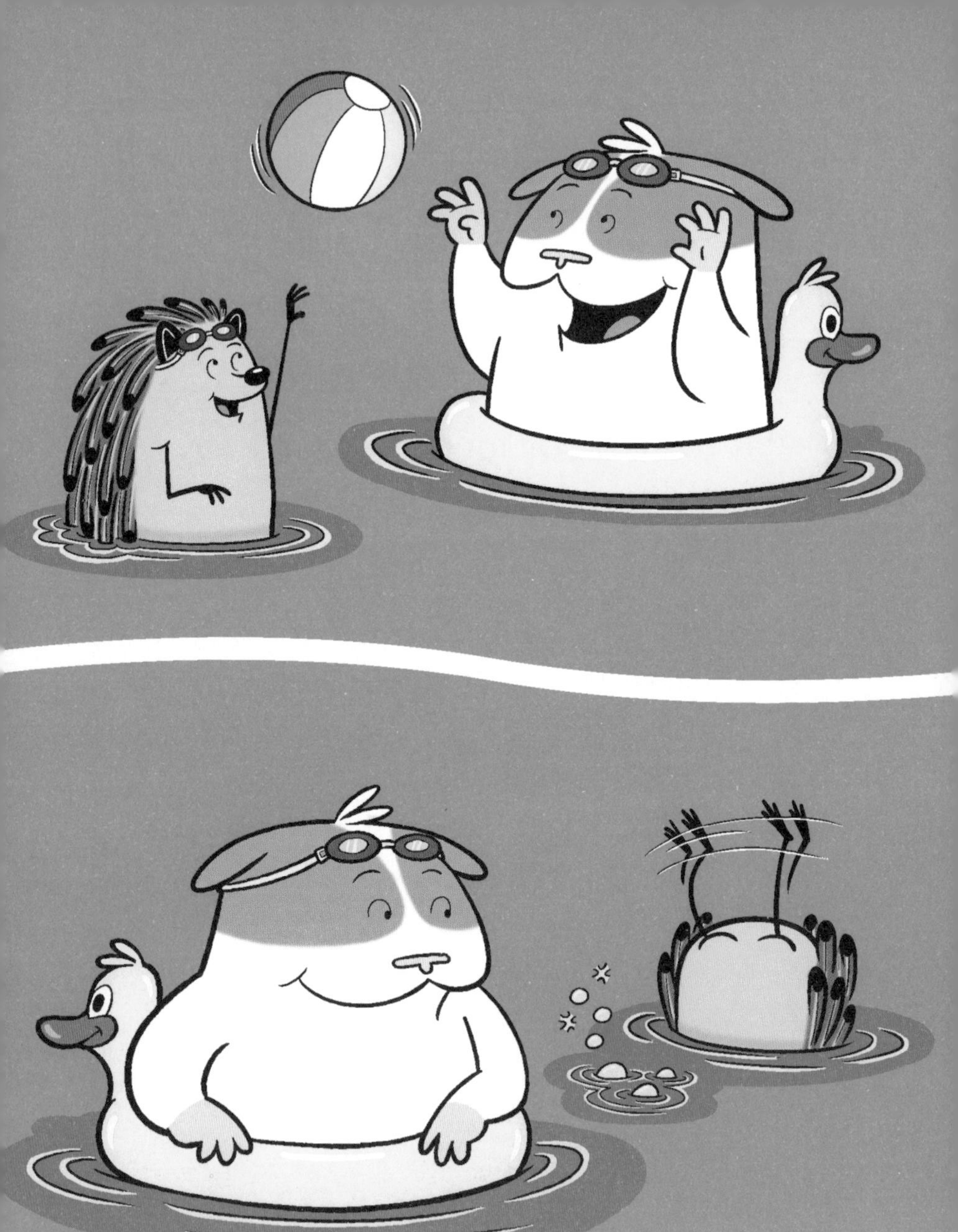

Haha!

This stone is the treasure.
We will take turns diving for it.
Splash!

19

Now it is your turn.

Wait!

What?

This game will not work.

Why not?

My ducky keeps me above the water.

20

22

24

Then, you can reach the stone without going all the way under.

You will only need to put your face in the water.

That is the scary part!

Yes. The trick is to hold your nose.

You just pinch your nose, take a deep breath, and —

Pinch.

Huff!

Splash!

Pinch.

Huff!

Splash!

Hooray!

I found a coin!

Wow! I did not think you would find **real** treasure!

Maybe there are **more**.

35

Good thing I brought my pad and crayons.

What are you writing?

You will see.

Good luck! I will meet you at the **X**!

This is so exciting!

Hmmm.

PLAYGROUND

You used your coin to buy us ice cream!

Yes! That was my secret plan.

Thank you, Harry!

You are welcome, Hedgehog.

About the Author

Norm Feuti lives in Massachusetts with his family, a dog, two cats, and a guinea pig. He is the creator of the newspaper comic strips **Retail** and **Gil**. He is also the author and illustrator of the graphic novel **The King of Kazoo**. **Hello, Hedgehog!** is Norm's first early reader series.

YOU CAN DRAW HARRY!

1. Draw a potato shape.

2. Draw the ears, hair, and two big bumps for the mouth!

3. Add legs, feet, and a tail. Give Harry a chin.

4. Draw a tube around his belly, and add two circles on his head for the goggles.

5. Give Harry arms, eyes, and a wide letter T for the nose. Then, give the ducky a beak, hair, and eyes.

6. Color in your drawing!

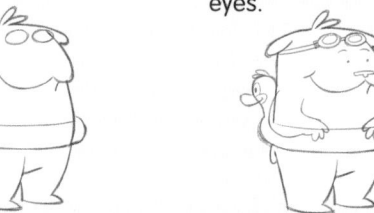

WHAT'S YOUR STORY?

Harry and Hedgehog like to play water games.
Imagine **you** play Dive for Treasure with them.
What treasures would each of you find?
What other games would you play?
Write and draw your story!